The Big Book of Animal Stories

Dick King-Smith

DICK KING-SMITH

The Big Book of Animal Stories

Published by the Penguin Group
Penguin Books Ltd, 27 Wrights Lane, London W8 5TZ, England
Penguin Putnam Inc., 375 Hudson Street, New York, New York 10014, USA
Penguin Books Australia Ltd, Ringwood, Victoria, Australia
Penguin Books Canada Ltd, 10 Alcorn Avenue, Toronto, Ontario, Canada M4V 3B2
Penguin Books (NZ) Ltd, Private Bag 102902, NSMC, Auckland, New Zealand

On the World Wide Web at: *www.penguin.com*

Penguin Books Ltd, Registered Offices: Harmondsworth, Middlesex, England

The Invisible Dog first published by Viking 1995; published in Puffin Books 1997
Clever Duck first published by Viking 1996; published in Puffin Books 1997
The Swoose first published by Viking 1993; published in Puffin Books 1994

This edition published by Viking 2000
3 5 7 9 10 8 6 4 2

Printed and bound in Great Britain by The Bath Press

British Library Cataloguing in Publication Data
A CIP catalogue record for this book is available from the British Library

ISBN 0–670–89357–9

Contents

THE
INVISIBLE DOG

DICK KING-SMITH

THE INVISIBLE DOG

Illustrated by Paul Howard

Contents

1. The Lead and Collar

Rupert died when Janie was only two, so that she didn't really remember anything about him.

She knew what he looked like, of course – there were lots of photos of him:

on his own, or with Mum or Dad, and one she specially liked of herself as a toddler sitting on the lawn with Rupert standing beside her. She was just sorry she'd never known him.

"Mum," Janie said one day, "how long ago did Rupert die?"

"Oh, let's see," her mother said. "He died when you were two and now you're seven. So – five years ago."

"And how old was he?"

"He was eight."

"That's not very old for a dog, is it?" Janie said.

"Not for most dogs," her mother said, "but then Rupert was very big, a giant really. Great Danes don't usually live as long as smaller dogs."

"What did he die of?"

"Kidney failure."

"Were you and Daddy sad?"

"Terribly."

"Is that why we've never had a dog since?"

"I suppose it is, really. We talked about getting a puppy, but somehow it seemed as though no other dog could replace Rupert, so we never did."

"What kind of puppy would you have got?" asked Janie.

"Oh, a Great Dane again, I think. We wouldn't want any other sort of dog. But they're awfully expensive to buy and awfully expensive to keep."

"Shall we ever have another one, d'you think?"

"I don't know, darling," Janie's mother said. "We'll see."

"We'll see", Janie knew, always meant "probably not and don't go pestering me about it or it'll be certainly not". So she thought she'd better drop the subject.

However, the spirit of the late great Rupert must have decided otherwise, for only a few days later Janie came by chance upon something she'd never set eyes on before.

She was hunting about at the back of the garage, where her father had his workbench, looking for an oil-can to oil her bike, when she saw something hanging high on a nail in a dark dusty corner.

It was a dog-collar with a lead attached.

Janie climbed up on to the bench and took it down.

The collar was a very big, broad, brass-studded one with a round metal disc attached to the buckle. She rubbed the disc clear of dust and there, scratched on the face, was the name RUPERT and, underneath, their telephone number.

Janie put the collar to her nose. It smelt

of leather and dog, and just for a
moment it made her feel sad to think that
this faint smell was all that was left of the
creature whose great neck the collar had
encircled. How many hundreds of times
in his eight years of life would he have
gone for a walk wearing it, with Mum or
Dad holding the end of the thick plaited
lead.

12

Janie went out of the garden gate and wandered up the lane, the loop of the lead in her left hand, the empty collar dangling. She looked down at the thick leather circlet and imagined the shape and sweep of the great neck, the Great Dane neck, within it. She saw the dog clearly in her mind's eye as it walked beside her.

Lost in a daydream, she almost bumped into Mrs Garrow, an elderly widow who lived alone in one of the cottages at the top end of the village.

"Hullo, Janie! Where are you off to then?" said the old lady with a loud laugh. Mrs Garrow's laugh sounded like nothing so much as a duck quacking.

"I'm taking my dog for a walk," Janie said.

"I can see that," said Mrs Garrow, and she put out a hand and patted the air behind the dangling collar, just where the dog's back would have been.

"Who's a good boy then?" said Mrs Garrow. "He's looking ever so well, Janie; you must be proud of him. Make sure you keep him on the lead, mind; there's a lot of traffic in the lane these days," and she went on her way, quacking loudly.

Some people never grow too old for games of make-believe, thought Janie. That's nice. And two can play at that.

"Heel!" she said, and she walked on, the invisible dog pacing at her side.

2. The Name

After Janie had gone to bed that night, her parents were talking.

"I see Janie's got hold of old Rupert's collar and lead," her father said.

"Yes," her mother said. "She's been carrying it around all day. It's lying beside her bed now."

"When I arrived home from work," her father said, "she was so engrossed with it I don't think she even heard the car. She was walking round the lawn, dangling the collar and talking away to an imaginary animal. Every now and then she'd stop and say 'Sit!' and then after a bit she'd say 'Heel!' and walk on again."

"I know. I can only think she must have a very vivid imagination to play a game like that for so long."

"Has she been pestering you to get a puppy?"

"No. It would be nice though, David, wouldn't it? One day."

"Another Great Dane?"

"Of course."

"Oh, come off it, Sally," Janie's father said. "They're awfully expensive to buy and awfully expensive to keep. I mean, these days a decent Dane puppy costs over three hundred pounds."

"You know that, do you?"

"Well . . . yes, I just happened to notice an advertisement. And as for feeding a growing pup – well, you can reckon on over six hundred pounds a year."

"So we can't afford one?"

"No. You weren't seriously thinking of getting one?"

"No."

"Right then."

At breakfast next morning they both noticed that the loop of the lead was round Janie's left wrist as she ate, the collar on the floor beside her.

"Do we have to have that dirty old thing at table?" her father asked.

"He's not a dirty old thing," Janie said.

"He? I'm talking about the collar and lead."

"Oh sorry, Dad, I thought you were talking about my dog."

"It's a funny thing," her mother said, "but Daddy and I can't actually *see* a dog."

"You wouldn't," said Janie. "He's invisible."

"I see."

"No you don't, Mum."

"I mean, I hear what you're saying. By the way, what do you feed him on?"

"Invisible food."

"In an invisible dish?"

"Naturally."

"Think of the money you're saving," Janie's father said, "never having to fork out for dog-meat or biscuits. Can't cost you a penny."

"Of course it does, Daddy. When we

go shopping today, you wouldn't believe
how much I shall have to spend."

"Invisible money?"

"Of course."

"Has he got a name, this invisible
dog?" her mother asked.

"Well, no, not yet," said Janie. "I haven't decided."

"Have you decided what breed he is?" her father said.

"Oh honestly, Daddy!" said Janie. "I should have thought that you'd have known a Great Dane when you saw one."

"You could just call him Rupert," her

mother said. "That's what's written on his collar, after all."

"No," said Janie. "I think this dog ought to have a different name, don't you?"

"Oh yes," they said.

"I mean, he's quite a different colour, isn't he?"

"Is he?" they said.

"Rupert was a fawn dog, with a black mask," Janie's father said.

"Whereas this one," Janie's mother said, "is . . . um . . . well . . . what would you say, Janie?"

"Black with white splodges," said Janie. "Or white with black splodges, whichever you like to say."

"A harlequin Great Dane!" they cried. "Of course."

"So he really needs a sort of black-and-white name, doesn't he?"

"Like Magpie, you mean?" said her mother.

"Or Zebra," said her father.

"Or Panda."

"Or Penguin."

"Yes," said Janie, "but I don't like any of those names. I think I'll just call him Spotty."

"You can't!" they cried with one voice. "You can't call a harlequin Great Dane 'Spotty'. It's not dignified enough."

"He's my dog," said Janie, and she put down a hand and stroked an invisible back, "so I can call you Spotty if I want to, or Tom, Dick or Harry."

"He liked 'Harry'," said Janie's father, looking down at the collar lying on the floor. "He wagged his tail a bit when you said 'Harry'."

Janie's mother raised her eyes to heaven.

22

"Oh honestly, David!" she said. "You're as bad as she is. No doubting where she gets it from."

"Harry," said Janie. "I quite like that."

"Or perhaps Henry," said her father. "That's a bit more dignified."

"Henry?" said Janie. "Henry! Yes, you're right, Daddy. He's wagging his tail like mad now. Henry it is!"

3. The Price

All this happened towards the end of the
holidays, and as the new term
approached, Janie's parents began to
wonder if Henry would be taken to
school.

They worried at the thought of their child doing lessons or playing games or eating her lunch, always attached to the lead and collar. It was all very well to make-believe at home, but whatever would the teachers think?

They waited, a little nervously, for the first day of term.

"Got all your school things ready?" her father said at breakfast.

"Yes."

Her mother drew a deep breath.

"You're not taking Henry, are you, darling?" she said.

"Oh honestly, Mummy!" said Janie. "You know we're not allowed pets at school, not even a gerbil, let alone a Great Dane. But he can come in the car with us, can't he?"

"Oh. Yes. Of course."

"And then he can go back home with

25

you once you've dropped Daddy off at the station."

"All right."

"You'll have to exercise him, Mum."

"Take him for a walk, d'you mean?" her mother asked nervously.

"No, just let him out for a run in the garden. Mind you take his lead off or he'll trip over it. Just let him out at lunch time, that'll be enough. After all, we don't want Henry making a mess in the house. Specially an invisible mess."

"I wonder what it would be like," said her father thoughtfully, "stepping in an invisible dog-mess?"

When, however, her mother drove to fetch Janie at the end of the school day, she found that she had forgotten something. As they came out of the playground and reached the car, parked

26

at the roadside, Janie looked in at the back seat and made a little noise of disappointment.

"Oh, Mum!" she said. "You left Henry at home."

Janie's mother stopped herself on the verge of saying, "No, he's there all right, it's just that he's invisible." From then on she was always careful, whenever she collected Janie, to have put the collar at one or other end of the back seat and the lead ready for Janie to clip on when they arrived home.

"Have you told them at school?" Janie's mum said, a few days later.

"Told who?"

"Your friends."

"What about?"

"About Henry."

"No. But I told our teacher," said Janie.

"What! That we'd got a Great Dane?"

"No. Just that we might have one, one day. Another one, I mean, as well as Henry."

"What makes you think that?"

"Well, we might, Mum, mightn't we? You never know what's going to happen."

"I do," her mother said, "and we aren't. Your father wouldn't consider it."

"How d'you know?"

"You ask him."

So when her father came home from work that evening, Janie did.

She didn't for one moment think that he'd say yes, though she half hoped for a "We'll see", which would mean there might be a chance, but he simply said, "No, of course not. Can't afford it."

"How much would a puppy cost

then?" Janie said. "A Great Dane puppy, I mean. A harlequin Great Dane."

Her father stopped himself on the verge of saying "three hundred pounds". Possibly that was a guess on the low side, he thought, and probably harlequins are more expensive than other colours, and anyway, if I say a really high price she'll forget the whole silly business.

"Five hundred pounds," he said.

Janie looked down at the collar, dangling as usual from its lead, and patted an invisible head.

"D'you hear that, Henry?" she said. "Just think what you must be worth."

"You stick to Henry," her father said.

"I could save up my pocket money," Janie said.

"Take you about ten years."

"Just think! I'd be seventeen," said

30

Janie, "nearly eighteen, and then I'd be grown up and you wouldn't be able to stop me buying a Great Dane puppy."

"I'm not stopping *you* buying one now," her father said. "Just so long as you've got the money. You come along with five hundred pounds and then . . ."

"And then what, Daddy?"

"Then we'll see."

4. The Show

Janie's birthday was in the early part of January, and for a treat each year she was always taken to London – to the Zoo, or Madame Tussaud's, or the Tower, or the Natural History Museum.

"What shall we do for Janie's birthday outing this year?" her mother said. "Can you think of something a bit out of the ordinary?"

"As a matter of fact, I can," Janie's father said.

"What?"

"Cruft's."

"Cruft's Dog Show?"

"Yes. Might be rather fun, don't you think?"

"Which day? It's a four-day show, I seem to remember.

"Oh, the fourth day, I think."

"Why? No, don't tell me, David; I can read you like a book. Great Danes are judged on the fourth day. That's it, isn't it?"

"Well, yes. I mean, I know they're your favourite breed, Sally."

"Not by any chance yours too?"

34

"Well, yes. But I just thought it might be fun for Janie."

"I see. Don't you think it might be a bit hard on the child? She may not be satisfied with an invisible Great Dane. It isn't as if you had any intention of buying a puppy."

"No," said her husband. "Though I told Janie *she* could buy one."

"You did *what*?"

"I said that if she came along with five hundred pounds clutched in her hot little hand, then I wouldn't stop her buying a Dane puppy."

"You say the stupidest things sometimes. Next thing you know, she'll be robbing a bank."

"Well, shall we go to Cruft's or shan't we?"

"Ask Janie."

"A dog show?" Janie said when the

idea was put to her. "What dog show?"

"Cruft's. The biggest of them all. There'll probably be something like 20,000 dogs there altogether. Of every breed."

"Great Danes?"

"Of course."

"Harlequin Great Danes like Henry?"

"Sure to be some. Though they'll look a bit different from Henry."

"Why?"

"Well, you can't see him too well."

"Can he come to Cruft's?"

"No."

"Poor old boy," said Janie, fondling an invisible ear. "I'll tell you all about it afterwards."

Apart from those old snapshots of Rupert, Janie had never in her life set eyes upon a Great Dane until that unforgettable day shortly after her eighth birthday. They had walked into the great hall of Olympia and made their way past the judging of a whole lot of other breeds – terriers and collies and gun dogs and many more – and suddenly there were the giants, a ring full of them.

Black and blue, fawn and brindle and harlequin, they stood and showed themselves in all their majestic dignity.

The judge was a little woman, small enough, it seemed to Janie, to have gone for a ride on any one of the great dogs whose points she was so carefully examining.

Janie and her mother and father watched at the ringside as class succeeded class, and handlers stood their charges before the little judge, or walked or ran around the ring, the huge dogs striding out beside them. Tall men or

short men, thin ladies or fat, old or
young, they each had something in
common, thought Janie – a Great Big
Beautiful Dane. If only we could have
one some day, she said to herself.

A man beside them noticed the rapt
expression on Janie's face.

"Bet you wish you had a dog like one of those," he said with a smile.

"Actually," said Janie, "I have. He's called Henry."

"Imagine that!" said the friendly man.

"Henry's rather out of the ordinary," Janie's mother said.

"Out of this world," said her father.

They stayed and watched till the end
of the judging, till the little woman had
made her choice between Best Dog and
Best Bitch. Both appeared equally
beautiful to Janie – every one of the
Danes there, it seemed to her, were
faultless; she couldn't see any difference
between them except colour. But she

desperately wanted the dog to win Best
of Breed because, just by chance, he was
a harlequin. And her wish was granted.

"He's beautiful!" Janie said.

"Isn't he just!"

"They all were."

"Weren't they just!"

Afterwards they went round the
benches, and there he was, with his
rosettes and his prize cards and his
proud owner.

Janie pushed between a small crowd of
admirers to get a closer look. The dog,
she could see, knew just what a clever
fellow he was. He had a kind of smile on
his great face and his long tail wagged
slowly and majestically.

"He's called Champion Larkmeadow
Nobleman of Merlincourt," she told her
parents.

"Gosh! What a mouthful."

"But his owner called him Bob. I heard him."

"That's better."

"Funny thing though," said Janie.

"What?"

"He looked just *exactly* like Henry."

5. The Tea-leaves

The postbox was at the top end of the village, not much more than a hundred yards from Janie's front gate. It was, in fact, set into the low garden wall of Mrs Garrow's cottage, and Janie sometimes wondered how the old lady posted any letters she might write. Did she come out into the lane and post them from the front like everyone else, or did she stay inside her garden and stretch over the wall, then feel for the opening in the box and post them, so to speak, upside down? No, she wouldn't be tall enough, would she?

One day she found the answer.

"Take this letter up to the post for me, Janie, will you please?" her mother had

said, and Janie set off, the letter in one
hand, the lead in the other, the collar
around Henry's invisible neck.

She was approaching the postbox
when she saw Mrs Garrow come out of
her front door, also carrying a letter, and
walk across her little bit of lawn to a spot
directly behind the bright red box.

She'll never be able to do it; she's too
short, Janie thought, but then Mrs
Garrow seemed suddenly to rise higher,
and she leaned right over the top of the
wall and posted her letter.

Straightening up, she saw Janie and let
out a burst of quacking laughter.

"Bet you thought I wasn't tall enough

to do that!" she said. "And I wouldn't be if it weren't for these," and Janie could see that the old lady was standing on top of a little pair of wooden steps positioned behind the wall.

"I always enjoy doing that, Janie," Mrs Garrow said. "'Specially as I always feel somehow that the postbox is mine, seeing as it's set in my wall."

"Oh," said Janie. "Is it all right if I post my letter in it?"

"Course it is!" cried Mrs Garrow with another volley of quacks. "Though I'm surprised to see *you* carrying it."

"What d'you mean?" Janie asked.

"Well, I'd have thought that great animal of yours would be carrying it for you in his mouth. Some dogs do, you know. My! He's a size, isn't he? What's his name?"

"Henry," said Janie.

"Well I never!" said Mrs Garrow. "D'you know what, Janie? That was my late husband's name."

"Oh," said Janie. "I'm sorry," she added.

"No need to be sorry, dear," said Mrs Garrow. "He's been dead and gone these twenty years, though never a day passes when I don't think of him. And you know what? There's a lot in common between your Henry and mine."

"How d'you mean?" Janie said.

"Well, my Henry was a great big chap too – he didn't need a step-ladder to post a letter – and another thing, he was quiet, just like your dog. He doesn't bark much, does he?"

"No," Janie said.

"Saw one just like him on the telly, couple of weeks ago," Mrs Garrow said. "Some big dog show it was."

"Cruft's!" said Janie. "We went there!"

"Did you take Henry?"

"No, but there was a dog there just exactly like him and it won the prize for Best of Breed. Another harlequin Great Dane, it was."

"A harlequin Great Dane, eh?" said Mrs Garrow, and she looked down from

her perch at the dangling collar and nodded.

"I see," she said.

"And Daddy says I can have a real one – I mean, another one – but only on one condition."

"And what's that?"

"I have to have five hundred pounds."

"That's a lot of money."

"It's a fortune!"

Mrs Garrow looked down at Janie and her invisible dog, and her wrinkled face creased some more, into a smile.

"Talking of fortunes, Janie," she said, "how would you like me to tell yours?"

"Oh, could you? Oh yes, please," said Janie.

"Come in and have a cup of tea then."

"I'd better ask Mum," said Janie.

"You do that," said Mrs Garrow. "I've got some nice cake."

When Janie returned, permission granted, Mrs Garrow called from her front door, "Come on in."

"What about Henry?" Janie said.

"He'd better stay in the garden," Mrs Garrow said. "My old black cat doesn't like dogs."

"All right," said Janie, and she came in through the gate and dropped the collar and lead on the lawn. "Down, Henry," she said, and "Stay."

"Now," said Mrs Garrow when they had drunk their tea, "let's have a look in your cup."

For a long moment she studied the tea-leaves in the bottom of the cup, very carefully.

Then she said, "Janie, I think you're going to be lucky."

"Why? What can you see?" Janie asked.

"Look," said Mrs Garrow, handing the cup back.

Janie looked in, but all she could see was a scatter of black tea-leaves at the bottom of the white cup.

"I can't see anything," she said.

"You've got to know what you're looking for," said Mrs Garrow. "There's a shape there all right – a great big shape

it is, no doubt about it, and what's more, it's black-and-white."

"A harlequin Great Dane!" cried Janie. "Is that what it is?"

Mrs Garrow smiled her crinkly smile.

"I shouldn't be surprised," she said. "And now you'd best get off home."

Out on the lawn, Janie picked up the end of the lead.

"Heel, Henry!" she said, and "Thank you for the tea, Mrs Garrow. I hope the tea-leaves were right."

"Talking of leaves," said Mrs Garrow, "this lawn's covered in them. I'd better sweep them up. Bye bye, Janie dear."

"Goodbye," Janie said.

For a moment she stood in the lane by the postbox, looking over the low wall. On the lawn old Mrs Garrow was sweeping away with a long broomstick of birch twigs, watched by her black cat.

6. The Money

"I'm bankrupt," said Janie's mother.

"And I soon shall be," said her father. "I don't think it's fair. Whoever heard of a dog playing Monopoly?"

"Specially an invisible dog," his wife said.

Janie sat grinning, a great stack of money in front of her. She patted the unseen head at her side.

"You played well," she said.

It had been Janie's idea that Henry should take part in the game. She threw the dice for him, of course, and moved his symbol round the board, and collected the rents from all his properties as well as her own. As always, she played with the top-hat, her mother with the flat-iron and her father with the car. Henry's symbol had naturally to be the dog.

"OK," said Janie's father as the car landed on Henry's Park Lane hotel. "I've had it too. You win, Janie. You and Henry."

"Cheer up, Daddy," Janie said. "I've got a nice surprise for you," and from a wad of money she peeled off a £500-note and held it out to him.

"What's this for?" he said.

"For my Great Dane puppy.

Remember what you said? 'You come along with five hundred pounds,' you said . . . "

"Oh, no you don't," her father said. "It's got to be real money if you want a real dog. Five hundred pounds of Monopoly money indeed – you'll be lucky!"

"I think I will be," Janie said.

Later, Janie's mother said, "I wish you hadn't done that silly thing, David."

"What silly thing?"

"Telling Janie she could have a puppy if she had five hundred pounds. You saw the look on her face just now – she genuinely believes she's going to be lucky. It's not fair on the child – there's no way she could find that amount. Either put up the money yourself or shut up about it."

"I just might," Janie's father said.

"Might what? Shut up?"

"No, put up the money. Ever since Janie brought out that lead and collar, I've found myself thinking of dear old Rupert and what a super dog he was and wondering why we never replaced him. And what with Cruft's – well, I must admit I'm getting quite keen on the idea. After all, Sally, we are the right sort of people to have a big dog – we've a sizeable house and garden, we live in the country, and we can afford it."

"You told Janie we couldn't when she first asked you."

"Yes, I know; it's all the fault of that invisible dog of hers. The more she plays that game, the more I find I want to see an actual living, breathing, flesh-and-blood Dane on that lead."

"A harlequin."

"Does that matter? Surely any colour would do."

"Not for Janie it wouldn't. And it may not be easy to find exactly what we want."

"We?" said her husband. "You go along with the idea then?"

"We'll see."

"We will," said Janie's father, and he grinned, slyly it seemed to his wife.

"What have you got up your sleeve?" she said.

"Not up my sleeve," said Janie's father. "In my pocket," and he took something out of it.

"What's that?"

"An advertisement. I cut it out of the local paper."

"You don't mean . . . ?"

"Yes. Listen. 'Great Dane puppies for sale. Blacks, blues, one harlequin.'"

"Price?"

"Doesn't say."

"Where?"

"Not all that far away. Extraordinary, isn't it? I had no idea there was a Great Dane breeder anywhere near here. And there's a harlequin in the litter too. What a bit of luck!"

"Janie said she'd be lucky, didn't she?"

"I know. All it needs now is for five hundred pounds to drop out of the sky and land in Janie's lap and I shall begin to believe in witchcraft."

At that instant they heard a loud noise outside.

64

"What on earth was that?" Janie's father said.

Her mother went to look out of the window.

"Oh, it's only old Mrs Garrow going down the lane," she said. "She has the most peculiar laugh."

"I'll say! I thought it was a duck quacking."

"She's chatting with Janie. And she's flapping her hand up and down. Oh no, I see what she's doing – she's patting Henry."

"That," said Janie's father, "has really made my mind up. If it's got to the stage where Janie's playing her invisible dog game with people like Mrs Garrow, it's high time we got a visible one."

"Will you tell Janie?"

"No, not yet. The harlequin pup may be sold, or it may be a bitch, or it may just be a poor specimen. We must go and see the puppies."

"When?"

"As soon as you've taken Janie to school tomorrow morning."

"But you'll be going to work."

"No. I'm taking the day off. I've fixed it at the office. Urgent business."

"David! You are a slyboots!"

The postman came just as Janie was getting ready to go to school next morning, and by the time their car reached the top end of the village his van was parked outside Mrs Garrow's cottage while he collected the outgoing mail from the postbox.

Mrs Garrow was chatting to him and she waved at Janie as they went by.

"Your friend," said Janie's mother.

"She's nice," said Janie, waving back.

"Did you enjoy going to tea with her?"

"Yes, it was interesting."

They drove on, while the postman got into his van and drove away, down towards their house.

7. The Kennels

Back home again, Janie's mother found her husband still sitting at the breakfast table, looking very pleased with life. He waved a letter at her.

"What's up?" his wife said. "You look as if you've won the pools."

"*I* haven't won anything," Janie's father said. "Janie has. Do you remember when she was very small I bought some Premium Bonds for her? Well, they've won her some money, quite a nice sum. Here's the letter telling me so."

"Don't tell me it's five hundred pounds!"

"No, that would be an unbelievable coincidence after what I said about buying a Great Dane puppy."

"How much then?"

"Two hundred."

"It won't be enough then," Janie's
mother said.

"Enough for what?"

"Why, to buy one of those puppies.
For Janie to buy one, I mean, with her
own money."

They looked at one another.

"We might have to add a bit to it,"
Janie's father said.

70

They looked at one another again, and they smiled.

"Ring up the kennels," Janie's mother said, "and see if they'll keep the harlequin until we get there."

She listened anxiously to her husband's share of the conversation.

"Good morning. I'm inquiring about the pups you advertised. Are they sold?"

. . .

"I see. But you still have the harlequin?"

. . .

"Dog or bitch?"

. . .

"Oh, good. That's the one we're interested in. Can you keep him for us?"

. . .

"Yes, I understand. We must take a chance on that. We'll be with you just as soon as we can. By the way, how much are you asking for him?"

The answer to this last question seemed to take some time, but at last Janie's father put the phone down.

"The harlequin is a dog puppy," he said, "and he's not sold. The woman said she couldn't guarantee to keep him for us. She's sold a couple of the others but hasn't had anyone after the harlequin yet."

72

"How much?" Janie's mother said. "She seemed to take a lot of time answering when you asked her that."

"That's because she was giving me a long spiel about how well bred this litter is, and what the mother had won, and the fact that the father is Champion Thingummy Nobleman of Wotsitsname – you know, the dog that won at Cruft's."

"So, how much?"

"Five hundred pounds."

"I'm awfully sorry," the breeder said when they arrived. "No sooner had you rung off than someone turned up, wanting the harlequin puppy. He's just this moment driven off; you probably passed him on your way here."

Janie's parents looked at one another once more, and they sighed a joint sigh.

"There are still two blacks and a blue left," said the breeder.

"No," Janie's mother said, "thanks all the same. It has to be a harlequin or nothing."

"Leave me your address and phone number then," said the breeder. "I might hear of something."

"At least Janie doesn't know anything

about it," said one to the other as they drove home again, "so she won't be disappointed."

"And she's got a nice surprise waiting for her when she gets back from school this afternoon."

"I didn't even know I had a Premium Bond," Janie said when they showed her the letter and the cheque. "You never told me."

"We don't tell you everything," her father said.

"Two hundred pounds!" Janie said. "Nearly enough to buy half a harlequin Great Dane puppy!"

"Has it really *got* to be a harlequin?" her mother said.

"Yes. She said so."

"Who said so?"

"Mrs Garrow."

"What on earth has Mrs Garrow got to do with it?"

"She saw it."

"I don't know *what* you're talking about," her father said.

After tea Janie took the invisible dog for a walk up the lane. As she passed Mrs Garrow's cottage, the old lady looked over the garden wall and said, "Hullo, Janie. Better luck next time."

I don't know what you're talking about, Janie thought.

"Ask your mum and dad," Mrs Garrow said, just as though she'd read Janie's mind.

"Ask them what?"

"Where they went this morning."

"Where did you go this morning?" Janie asked when she got home again.

"How d'you know we went anywhere?" her father said.

"I just do."

There was a pause.

"Tell her," her mother said.

At that moment the phone rang. It was the Great Dane breeder.

"I've just this minute had a thought," she said. "Since you just missed that puppy this morning and are set on having a harlequin, I've had an idea, if you're interested. I have a nine-month-old harlequin dog that might do you. He's a good typical specimen, with a

lovely nature, but he has a fault that spoils him for the show-ring."

"What sort of fault?" Janie's mother said.

"He's got a kink in his tail – a little sort of twist near the end of it. He was born like that, but I've kept him on because he's such a lovable character. Would you like to see him?"

They arrived once more at the kennels, this time with Janie. The breeder looked at her as she stood, lead in hand, collar dangling. "That's a biggish collar," she said. "Have you had a Dane before?"

"We had one called Rupert," Janie said, "when I was very small, but he was fawn, not a harlequin like this one."

"Which one?" said the breeder.

"Janie has an invisible dog," her father said. "He goes everywhere with her. He's never any trouble."

80

"Sit, Henry!" Janie said.

"Did you say Henry?" said the
breeder. "How extraordinary! Hang on
half a tick, I'll fetch the dog."

Of course they all fell in love with him
at first sight. Already he seemed
enormous, with feet like soup-plates. He

did not squirm or wriggle as a puppy would have done, but stood steady in black-and-white dignity as befitted someone who was almost grown-up.

"His nose is partly black and partly pink!" Janie's father said as the young dog sniffed at them.

"That's all right," the breeder said. "A harlequin's allowed a butterfly nose."

"And he's got one brown eye and one blue!" said Janie's mother, as he smiled at them.

"A wall eye. That's all right too. He's a good typical specimen, with a lovely nature, but, like I said, he has a kink in his tail – that little sort of twist near the end of it."

As if he understood, the dog slowly wagged his tail.

"I like that," Janie said. "I want to buy him, please."

"*You* want to?" the breeder said, smiling. "Have you got enough money of your own, d'you think?"

"I've got two hundred pounds," Janie said.

"I won't charge you that much," the breeder said. "As I told you, he's no good for show, with that fault. But I don't think I can give him to you – he's cost me a lot to rear. On the other hand, I feel sure that you'll give him a really good home. So shall we say a hundred pounds?"

Janie put out a hand.

"It's a deal," she said. "What's he called?"

"You aren't going to believe it," the breeder said. "In fact I must confess that there's something very strange about all this. But he's called Henry."

Janie nodded. It was as though she had expected this news.

Carefully she unbuckled the collar from the invisible dog and fastened it again around the neck of his successor. "Good boy, Henry," she said.

8. The Twist

About a week later Janie came out of the
front gate and turned up the lane, the
lead in her right hand, her dog walking
steadily at heel with his long strides, his
great head not far below her shoulder.
From the buckle of his collar hung a new
round metal disc that said, above the
telephone number, HENRY.

They walked up the village until they came to Mrs Garrow's wall, with the red postbox set into it, and Janie opened the garden gate and went in. Inside the porch of the cottage were Mrs Garrow's wellies and, leaning in the corner, the long broomstick that she used for sweeping up leaves. Her cat sat on the mat.

"My old black cat doesn't like dogs," Mrs Garrow had said, but to Janie's surprise it stood up and began to rub itself against one of Henry's long legs, purring loudly. Henry looked embarrassed.

Janie knocked on the front door, and after a moment old Mrs Garrow opened it, smiling her crinkly smile.

"Hullo," Janie said. "This is Henry."

"I know that, dear," said Mrs Garrow. "You showed him to me before, lots

of times, don't you remember?"

She patted the dog.

"Who's a good boy then?" she said.
"He's looking ever so well, Janie. You
must be proud of him."

"I am," Janie said. "D'you see, he's
got a butterfly nose and a wall eye?

87

There's only one thing meant to be wrong with him though I don't think it matters a bit, and that's the twist in his tail."

"It was all in the tea-leaves," Mrs Garrow said.

"I don't understand," Janie said. "How can you know these things?"

Mrs Garrow let out her usual volley of quacks.

"Aha, Janie my dear!" she said. "That's the twist in the tale."

Clever Duck

DICK KING-SMITH

Clever Duck

Illustrated by Mike Terry

Contents

1. "Ignoramus"

"Ignoramuses!" said Mrs Stout. "That's what they are. Ignoramuses, every one of them."

"Who, dear?" asked her friend, Mrs Portly.

"Why, the other animals on this farm, of course."

"Leaving aside us pigs, you mean?" said another friend, Mrs O'Bese.

"Naturally, Mrs O'Bese," replied Mrs Stout. "All pigs are born with a high degree of intelligence, that goes without saying." There came grunts of agreement from the other sows – Mrs Chubby, Mrs Tubby, Mrs Swagbelly and Mrs Roly-Poly – as they rooted in the mud of their paddock.

"I am speaking," went on Mrs Stout, "of such creatures as the cows . . ."

"Dullards!" put in Mrs Chubby.

". . . and the sheep . . ."

"Simpletons!" said Mrs Tubby.

". . . and the chickens . . ."

"Morons!" said Mrs Swagbelly.

". . . and the ducks."

"Idiots!" cried Mrs Roly-Poly. "Imbeciles! Half-wits! Dimwits! Nitwits!"

"Just so," said Mrs Stout. "Each and every other creature on the farm is, as I said, an ignoramus. Why, there's not one of them that would even know what the word meant."

"Surely, dear," said Mrs Portly, "they couldn't be that stupid?"

"There's one sure way to find out," said Mrs O'Bese.

Unlike the others, Mrs O'Bese was an Irish pig, with an Irish sense of humour, and it struck her that here was a chance for a bit of fun.

On one side of the sows' paddock was a field in which the dairy herd was grazing, and Mrs O'Bese made her way up to the fence, close to which one of the cows stood watching her approach.

"Good morning," said Mrs O'Bese.

"Good moo-ning," said the cow.

"Are you," asked Mrs O'Bese, "an ignoramus?"

"Noo," said the cow. "I'm a Friesian."

Mrs O'Bese went to a second side of the paddock, where there was a field full of sheep, and spoke to one.

"Hey, ewe!" she said.

"Me?" said the sheep.

"Yes, you. Who did you think I was talking to?"

"Ma?" said the sheep.

Some mothers do have 'em, thought the sow.

"Ignoramus," she said.

"Baa," said the sheep.

"D'you know what it means?"

"Na, na," said the sheep.

"Well," said Mrs O'Bese, "that cow over there is one and you are too."

"Na, na," said the sheep. "Me not two. Me one."

Mrs O'Bese shook her head so that her ears flapped.

"Ass," she grunted.

"Na, na," said the sheep. "Me ewe."

On a third side of the paddock was an orchard with a duckpond in it. A flock of chickens was pecking about under the apple trees, and there was a number of ducks, some walking around, some swimming in the pond.

Mrs O'Bese addressed a hen.

"Ignoramus," she said.

"What?" said the hen.

"Ignoramus. That's what you are, isn't it?"

"I don't get you," said the hen.

"It's a word," said Mrs O'Bese, "used to describe someone who has very little knowledge."

"Knowledge?" said the hen. "What does that mean?"

Mrs O'Bese sighed.

"How many beans make five?" she said.

The hen put her head on one side, consideringly.

"What's a bean?" she said.

"Oh, go and lay an egg!" said Mrs O'Bese.

"OK," said the hen, and went.

A duck waddled past.

I'll try a different approach, thought the Irish sow. Maybe I've been too abrupt. I'll turn on the charm, a bit of the old blarney.

"Top of the mornin' to ye, me fine

friend!" she cried. "Would you be after sparin' me a minute of your valuable time?"

The duck stopped. It was an ordinary sort of bird, brown and white in colour, and looking, Mrs O'Bese thought, as stupid as all its kind. It stared at her with beady eyes.

Then it said, "Quack!"

At this moment Mrs O'Bese heard the sound of heavy bodies squelching through the mud, and looked round to see that Mrs Stout and Mrs Portly, Mrs Chubby, Mrs Tubby, Mrs Swagbelly and Mrs Roly-Poly were all standing behind her.

"Listen to this," she grunted softly at them, and to the duck she said, loudly and slowly as one does to foreigners, "Now then, my friend. I wonder if perhaps you'd be able to help me.

104

There's this long word I've heard and I'm just a silly old sow, so I don't know the meaning of it."

"Quack!" said the duck again.

"The word," said Mrs O'Bese, "is 'ignoramus'."

"Is that so?" said the duck.

"Yes. Can you tell me what it means?"

"I must say," said the duck, "you surprise me. I had been under the distinct impression that pigs were reasonably intelligent. If you don't know what an ignoramus is, then you must be one."

2. Ed-u-cation

The seven sows stood in shocked silence
as the duck waddled away.

Then a black-and-white sheepdog
came trotting across the orchard and
approached the duck, tail wagging.

"Good morning, Damaris," said the
dog.

"It was a good morning, Rory," said
the duck, "until just now. Those sows!
They are *so* patronizing. They think that
they're so intelligent and that the rest of

us are fools. They need to be taught a lesson."

Rory stared thoughtfully at the sows.

"You're right, Damaris," he said, "I wouldn't mind wiping those smug smiles off their fat faces. I'll think of something."

"I'm sure you will, Rory," said Damaris. "You're miles cleverer than them anyway. I should know. If it hadn't been for you, I'd just be an ordinary duck."

An ordinary duck Damaris certainly was not. That is to say, she was not stupid and thoughtless and empty-headed as most ducks are. On the contrary, she was educated, and her teacher had been Rory. It had happened like this.

All sheepdogs are born with the instinct for herding things, and they begin as soon as they can run around. Rory as a puppy had often come into the orchard, practising his craft upon the chickens and ducks. The hens squawked and flapped and ran out of his way, but the ducks were slower moving and tended, like sheep, to bunch together, and, like sheep, to protest loudly at being forced to go this way and that.

Usually they managed to make their way to the pond, where the puppy could not follow, but one morning he came upon a mother duck with a brood of baby ducklings, and Rory set himself to keep these little ones away from the water.

For some time he moved them here and there, while the duck quacked distractedly in the background, but then a strange thing happened. One of the ducklings flatly refused to move any further. It simply sat down in the grass, seemingly unafraid of what must have appeared to it a very large animal, while the rest hurried off to join their mother.

The puppy sniffed at the duckling.

"What's the matter?" he said.

"The matter," piped the duckling, "is that you're a big bully and I'm tired."

"I was only practising," said Rory.

"What for?"

109

"Herding sheep. That's what I shall be doing. When I'm grown up. I'm a sheepdog, you see. My name's Rory. What's yours?"

"Damaris," said the duckling.

"That's a nice name," said Rory.

Ducks were silly animals, he knew that, his mother had told him, but this one seemed quite sensible.

"Look, Damaris," he said, "I'm sorry if I've upset you. Like I said, I have to practise – it's all part of my education."

"Ed-u-cation?" said the duckling. "What does that mean?"

"Why, learning things, being taught things you wouldn't otherwise know."

"Who teaches you?" asked Damaris.

"My mum. Doesn't your mum teach you?"

Does she, Damaris thought? She didn't teach me to swim, I did that on my own,

110

and the same with walking or running or eating or speaking. Yet here was this dog being taught things, like herding sheep. I don't suppose I could do that, but, all the same, it would be nice to have a proper – what was it? – education. I wonder – could Rory teach me?

And, indeed, that was how things turned out.

That first meeting between puppy and duckling led, as time went by, to a regular friendship between dog and duck.

Every day the young Rory would come and spend time with the young Damaris, and pass on to his friend all the things that he had learned. And because dogs – and especially sheepdogs – are highly intelligent creatures, and perhaps because Rory was a particularly bright sheepdog, and certainly because Damaris

was most anxious to learn about the world in a way no duck had ever done before, teacher and pupil worked wonderfully well together.

One day, about a year after their first meeting, the two friends were chatting together out in the orchard. Conversation was something they much enjoyed, something that was denied the other ducks, who only ever spoke to one another in monosyllables.

"Grub up" (when the farmer brought

their food), "Nice day" (when it was pouring with rain), and suchlike brief sentences were the limits of their conversational powers.

"In the matter of intelligence," Damaris said, "to which creature on the farm would you give the highest marks?"

Rory yawned.

"Me," he said.

"Dogs in general, you mean?"

"Yes."

"And the lowest?"

"Your lot, I suppose," said Rory.

"Ah," said Damaris. "So I am one of the stupidest creatures on the farm?"

Rory got to his feet, tail wagging.

"No, Damaris," he said. "You're different. You are a clever duck."

3.   A Lovely Little Scheme

Now, in summer-time some months
later, as they stood and looked at the
seven sows, Rory said, "Why have you
got your feathers in a twist anyway?
What did they say to you?"

"One of them asked me the meaning
of a word," said Damaris. "Pretended
she didn't know it. I was watching her
before, going round to the cows and to
the sheep, and she spoke to a hen too,
tried it on all of them, I bet."

"What word?" said Rory.

"'Ignoramus'. As if I didn't know."

"Typical," said Rory. "Trying to make other animals feel small. I've got a good mind to go out there and bite one or two of their fat backsides. Oh, they're so smug!"

"Look!" said Damaris. "There's another one coming to join them."

"That's the boar," said Rory, "and that's exactly what he is."

"How d'you mean?"

"Haven't you ever heard him? Wordy, pompous, opinionated, thinks he's always right about everything, never listens to anyone else. The sows are bad enough, but he's the biggest bore of the lot. Listen to him now – grunt, grunt, grunt, snort, snort – what rubbish he's talking."

In fact, the boar was indulging in his

usual reply to his wives' usual greeting.
The registered name on his pedigree was
Firingclose General Lord Nicholas of
Winningshot, but the sows simply called
him General.

"Good morning, General," they all
said as he came squelching up through
the churned-up paddock. Then, with an
inward sigh, each one of them tried hard
to put her mind into neutral, knowing
only too well what was coming.

"Ah, ladies," said the General in his deep voice. "Once again I find that I must question your customary greeting. There is no doubt that it is morning, but what precisely do you mean by 'good'? Virtuous? Pious? Kind? Well behaved? Worthy?"

"Sure and it isn't raining, General," said Mrs O'Bese.

"But," said the General, "is the absence of rainfall in itself good? Observe, for example, yonder duck, which to my surprise is consorting with a dog, an unlikely partnership in my opinion, of mammal and bird, of predator and prey, of . . . what was I saying?"

"Yonder duck," said Mrs Stout.

"Ah yes," said the General, "I recall. We were discussing the word 'good'. Such a beautiful morning as this may be good for us pigs, but I think, ladies, that we all know what kind of weather best pleases ducks."

"Rain," said Mrs Portly, Mrs Chubby, Mrs Tubby, Mrs Swagbelly and Mrs Roly-Poly in tones of deepest boredom.

"Exactly," said the General.

He moved ponderously towards the orchard fence.

"Now then," he said, "I hope that all you ladies realize, thanks to my brief explanation, that what is a 'good' morning for a pig may not be a 'good' morning for a duck. Have I made myself clear?"

There was no reply, and the boar turned round to see that the seven sows had made themselves scarce.

"See what I mean?" said Rory. "He's bored 'em all to tears."

"Oh Rory!" Damaris cried. "He's

worse than the sows! I don't know how
they can stand him."

"I don't know how we stand the lot of
them," said Rory. "Not all farmers keep
pigs, you know, Mum told me. We're
just unlucky."

Damaris was silent for a while,
thinking.

120

Then she said, "You spoke of 'keeping' pigs. Well, that means managing them, looking after them, feeding them and so forth, I know that. But it also means keeping them *in*, doesn't it? There's pig-netting all round their paddock. But down the other end, near the road, there's a gate."

Rory sat up abruptly.

"You mean . . . ?" he said.

"I mean," said Damaris, "that if somehow or other that gate was to be opened, then those patronizing sows and that pontificating boar might just . . . what's the word I'm looking for?"

". . . emigrate!" cried Rory. "Damaris, you're a genius! Let's go and have a look at that gate right now. Race you!" and away he ran.

Damaris flew direct across the muddy pig paddock, but so speedy was the

sheepdog that they arrived at the gate at
much the same time. Rory stood on his
hindlegs to examine its fastening. Then
he dropped back down with a growl of
disappointment.

"Hopeless!" he said. "There's a special
sort of bolt we could never pull back, and
worse, it's padlocked."

Damaris ducked under the metal gate, whose bars were too close together to admit more than a pig's snout. She splattered about in the mud, testing it with her bill.

"We don't need to open the gate," she said.

"Oh, look," said Rory, "ducks may fly, but pigs can't. How are they going to get over it?"

"Under it," Damaris said.

"They're far too big."

"Not if a hole was dug under the gate," said Damaris. "A great big hole. In this nice soft earth. By you."

4. Pigs Stopped Play

Very early the following morning, Rory did indeed dig that hole. Then he woke the pigs and said to the boar, very respectfully, "Would you be good enough to follow me, sir?"

At the gate he said, "Be kind enough to put your head under here, sir, and give a heave."

And, as the sows watched, the General put his great head in the hole and gave an almighty heave. Up came the gate, right off its hinges at one end, while at the other end, the bolt bent and the padlock snapped. Then down crashed the whole thing and away down the road went the sows, marching behind their master.

Before long there were grumblings of discontent in the ranks.

"I'm tired" and "My feet hurt" and "I'm starving hungry" and "I've had about enough of this", the sows complained, and finally the fattest of them, Mrs Roly-Poly, simply lay down in the road. Firingclose General Lord Nicholas of Winningshot heard the patter of hoofs cease behind him, and turned to see that all the sows had stopped.

"What is this?" he grunted. "Is this mutiny?"

"Don't know what the place is called, General," said Mrs Chubby, "but we're not going any further, not till we've had a rest and a bite to eat. My trotters is fair wore out.''

This brought from the General a long lecture, very military in tone, on duty and discipline, and for a while the sows lay in the road, not listening to a word, but simply resting and getting their breath. But when the boar paused to get his, Mrs Tubby said, ''Don't forget, General, that an army marches on its stomach.''

The General glowered at her. Then it occurred to him that his own stomach was feeling remarkably empty.

"Mrs Tubby," he said, "you took the words right out of my mouth. I was merely waiting until we found a suitable source of food," and, after a short lecture on the importance of a balanced diet, he set off again, the sows reluctantly following.

Not half a mile on, they came upon an open gateway and, beyond it, a fine crop of sugar-beet.

Eagerly the hungry pigs fell upon this bonanza, tearing and swallowing the green leafy tops and ripping great chunks out of the sweet roots in the ground beneath, eating and eating until at last they could hold no more, and even the General was speechless.

They lay in the ruined crop and

snored, and none of them saw a brown-and-white duck flying over the sugar-beet field.

"Looks like they've struck it lucky," Damaris told Rory when she arrived back at the farm. "Took me a bit of time, but when I did find them, they'd gorged themselves in a field of roots and were all lying there, blown out like balloons."

"Good," said Rory. "The happier they are, the less they'll want to come back here. We don't want things to go wrong for them so that they start to wish they were safely back in their old paddock."

But it was not long before things started to go very wrong indeed for the General and his wives.

At first it looked as though he had led them to the promised land, so well did they feed. For a day and a half they stuffed themselves with sugar-beet and sugar-beet tops. There was even a pond in the corner of the field, where they could drink and wallow. But then they began to pay the price.

"I don't know why, dear," said Mrs Portly to Mrs Stout, "but my guts don't half feel funny."

"Mine too," said Mrs Stout, and the other sows grunted agreement.

Mrs O'Bese did not mince her words.

"I've got the trots," she said, and before long they all had, the General included.

"In my opinion," he said uncomfortably, "this unfortunate condition has been caused by an imprudent consumption of the fresh green tops of the sugar-beet, acting as a purgative."

"Tops or bottoms," said Mrs O'Bese, "I know which end of me is worse off.

Come on, General, let's be getting out of here."

So they did, marching off once more down the road and leaving upon its surface plentiful evidence of their troubles.

But worse was to come.

That afternoon the pigs reached the outskirts of a village. So far their journey had been through a countryside of few houses and isolated farms, but now they came upon a signpost, saying

MUDDLEHAMPTON ½

and shortly after that there was another open gateway with a notice-board fixed upon it that read

MUDDLEHAMPTON CRICKET CLUB
PRIVATE
TRESPASSERS WILL BE
PROSECUTED

But just how prosecuted they were about to be, the General and his followers were yet to realize.

Beset by their troubled stomachs, the sows turned in at the gateway. Beyond, they could see, was a large and well-mown field with, at its far end, a single-storeyed wooden building before which a lot of people were sitting in deck-chairs.

In the middle of the field was a number of other people all dressed in white.

As the pigs drew nearer, they could see one of these white-clad people appear to throw an object at another, who struck at it with a kind of wooden cudgel. The spectators began to clap, and there were cries of "Good shot!" and "Well hit!", while the umpire at the bowler's end prepared to signal what looked like a certain four. But before the ball could reach the boundary, it reached the General, who fielded it neatly in his great jaws and started thoughtfully to chew it. Meanwhile, the sows began to root about in the well-kept grass, ploughing their way purposefully towards the pitch, while the shocked players stood as though turned to stone.

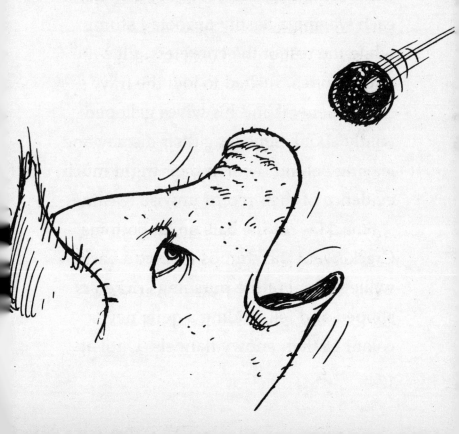

All eyes were on the pigs. No one noticed a brown-and-white duck circling overhead.

Then pandemonium broke loose as both the Muddlehampton First XI, who were fielding, and the two visiting batsmen sprang into action. The visitors led the charge, brandishing their bats, while with them ran six of the fielders, each waving a hastily uprooted stump, while the rest of the cricketers, plus the two umpires, rushed to join the fray.

The General and his wives galloped wildly about, squealing their dismay and leaving behind them in their fright much evidence of their recent unwise feasting.

Smack! went the bats on fat bottoms, Crack! went the stumps on broad backs, while several of the pursuing cricketers slipped and fell, adding a quite new colour to their snowy flannels. Until at last the invaders were driven out, and the match abandoned.

Muddlehampton's scorer was a stickler for the truth, and solemnly he wrote in his scorebook

PIGS STOPPED PLAY.

5. Mr Crook

After the scene on the cricket ground,
Damaris had not returned to the farm.
She was a fair-minded bird and,
annoying though she had thought the
pigs in the past, she began to feel sorry
for them as they hurried off, now sore
outside as well as inside. I must keep an
eye on them for as long as I can, she
thought. Perhaps someone else will give
them a home.

And, shortly, someone else did.

Among the spectators at the cricket match had been a local livestock dealer called Crook, a name, some said, that suited him well, for some of his deals were a trifle shady.

As the General and his wives retreated, squealing, before the onslaught of bat and stump, Mr Crook wasted no time, but slipped behind the pavilion and out of the ground, making his hasty way across the fields to his yard a little distance beyond the village. Thus it was that the angry sows (for by now each blamed the General for her bellyaches and her bruises) and their defeated leader heard a familiar and most welcome sound.

"Pig! Pig! Pig! Pig!" crooned Mr Crook, appearing in the lane before them, rattling a bucket, and the General and his wives eagerly followed. In through a gate

137

they went, across a yard, and into a
loose-box.

As Mr Crook closed the lower part of
the stout door behind them and bolted it,
he heard a quacking, and, looking up,
saw a brown-and-white duck flying
around.

He thought nothing of it, for he was
too busy reckoning in his head what a
Large White boar and seven sows,

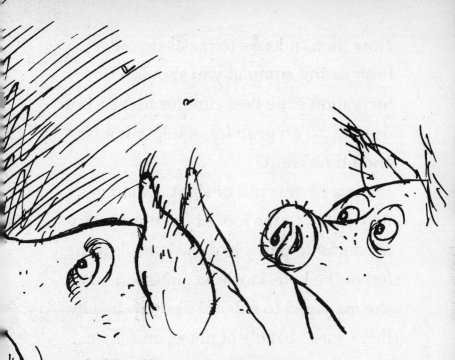

probably all in-pig, might fetch. He
leaned on the half-door and addressed
them.

"You lot can stop here," he said, "till
the fuss has died down, and if your
owner should come looking, I'll just say I
was keeping you safe for him. Then,
after a while, I'll take you to market, not
the local one, but a good way away.
Easiest money I've made in a long time.

Now then, it looks to me as if you've been eating summat you shouldn't. Starvation's the best cure for that sort of trouble, so no grub for you lot for a bit," and off he went.

Once he was out of sight, Damaris flew down to the loose-box. It isn't easy for ducks to perch like chickens, but the top of the half-door was quite wide, and she managed to balance upon it. Inside, there was a babble of noise, and it was plain to Damaris, listening, that the General was no longer in command.

"Now look what you've got us into," said one sow.

"First you walk the legs off us!"

"Then you let us eat all those sugar-beet tops!"

"And we get the trots!"

"Then we get beaten black and blue with clubs and sticks!"

"And finish up in this poky little hole!"

"With nothing to eat!"

"Ladies! Ladies! Please!" snorted the boar, but they took no notice of him.

"Calls himself a general," someone said. "A general disaster, he is!"

Not until the rumpus had died down did the sows notice Damaris perching on the half-door.

"Begorrah," said Mrs O'Bese, "isn't that the duck that knew the meaning of 'ignoramus'? She's a clever duck, that one is."

"Thank you," said Damaris.

She rather liked Mrs O'Bese, she suddenly realized, partly because of what she had just said, and partly because of the Irishness of her. Her heart, Damaris felt, was warmer than those of the others.

"Isn't it the lucky duck you are," went on Mrs O'Bese. "You can just fly home tonight. I wish I could. I wish we were all back home, well fed and housed in our old paddock, free to roam around and root about in the fresh air, instead of being stuck in this prison."

And a secure prison it looked to be. The floor was of concrete, and the strong wooden door, which opened inward, was faced with a large sheet of tin. No pig would ever be able to force it open.

"I'm beginning to feel sorry for them," Damaris said to Rory next morning, when she had told him all that had happened.

"I don't care about the pigs," said Rory, "but I'm beginning to feel sorry for the farmer. He's worried stiff, you can see it, driving about all over the place, every minute he can spare, looking for them."

"What are we to do?" said Damaris.

"We're going to have to tell the farmer where they are."

"Oh yes, and just how do we do that?"

Just then there came a shrill whistle.

"Here we go," said Rory. "You think of something, Damaris. If anyone can, you can."

Luvaduck, thought Damaris, I'm not *that* clever.

The farmer and his wife were sitting at breakfast the next morning.

"Where are you going to look today then, Jim?" asked the farmer's wife.

"Don't really know, Emma," said the farmer. "I've been everywhere – Muddlehampton, Muddlebury, Muddlechester, Upper Muddle, Lower Muddle."

At that moment they heard a tapping noise, and there, sitting on the window-sill outside and banging on the pane with her bill, was a brown-and-white duck.

"Whatever's she doing that for, silly

thing?" said the farmer's wife.

"Oh, that's Rory's pal, that is. Thick as thieves, they are. Never known a dog chum up with a duck before. You'd have thought Rory would have had more sense," said the farmer, and he rose and threw up the sash-window.

"What do you want, stupid?" he said.

For answer, Damaris let out a volley of excited quacks and flew away in the direction of Muddlehampton, calling loudly all the time.

"Perhaps she's trying to tell you something, Jim," said the farmer's wife.

"Oh, come on, Emma!" he replied. "Next thing you'll be saying she knows where the pigs are," and he shut the window.

Looking back, Damaris could see that no notice had been taken of her signals.

That afternoon Damaris flew all the way back to Mr Crook's yard and landed once again on top of the half-door of the loose-box. The pigs, she saw, now had a thick bed of straw, so that at least they looked a good deal cleaner.

"Hallo," she said. "How are things?"

"Terrible!" said a chorus of voices. "There's no room to move in here."

"Not even to swing the proverbial cat," said the General. "I fear that some of us are . . . what shall I say . . . getting upon each other's nerves."

"You're getting on everyone's nerves!" the sows shouted at him.

"See here, clever duck," said Mrs O'Bese. "Can you not help us?"

"I've tried," Damaris said, "but I can't think of a way."

"You wouldn't," said Mrs Stout. "You're not intelligent enough."

"Quite right, dear," said Mrs Portly.

Just then Damaris heard the noise of a door shutting on the other side of the yard.

147

There Mr Crook used a shed as his office, and, looking through its window, he saw a duck perched on the half-door of the loose-box. Mr Crook was very fond of ducks (with apple sauce and garden peas and new potatoes), and now he came out into the yard with his shotgun.

Damaris turned her head to see the man carrying what looked like a thick stick under his arm, and she took off and flew hurriedly up. Hardly had she aimed herself in the direction of home than she heard a tremendous bang and felt, all at the same time, the blast of the charge of shot as it whistled by her and a sudden agonizing pain in one wing.

6. The *Pig Breeders' Gazette*

There had been only one thought in Damaris's head and that had been of flight, to get away, as quickly and as far as possible, from the menace of the man with the gun. But flight was now beyond her powers.

Unbalanced, beating wildly but fruitlessly with her one good wing, Damaris tumbled out of the sky.

Yet she was destined to be lucky.

Through the valley in which all the

villages lay ran the River Muddle, and into it, mercifully, Damaris now fell with a great splash. Though she could no longer fly, she could swim, and she paddled hastily away.

So that by the time Mr Crook reached the river bank, intending to finish off his wounded prey, Damaris was nowhere to be seen.

Again by luck, the farm lay

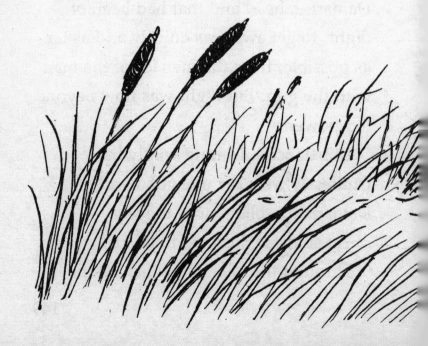

downstream from Muddlehampton so
that she was swimming with the current.
But after some time her homing instincts
told her that soon she would be carried
too far. I can't fly, she said to herself,
and there's no point in swimming any
further or I shall end up in the sea, so I
must get out and walk.

Normally she would have made for
home the shortest way – as the crow, or,

in this case, the duck, flies. But that
would have meant tramping across
country through hedges and over fences
and standing crops, so she went as a
human would have done, by road. And
still, as if to make up for misfortune, her
luck held. Ducks are some of the world's
worst walkers, and after almost a mile of
waddling, Damaris was tiring rapidly,

her injured wing throbbing, her legs aching, her head beginning to spin, when she heard the sound of an approaching motor.

There, coming towards her, was the farmer's pick-up truck.

As it reached her, it stopped and Rory leaped down from the back and ran to her.

"What's the matter?" he said.

"I've been shot," said Damaris.

"What's the matter, Rory?" called his mother Tess.

"She's been shot," said Rory.

"What's the matter, duck?" said the farmer, getting down from his cab.

"I've been shot," quacked Damaris, and "She's been shot" barked the two sheepdogs, but, of course, he did not understand. She was hurt though – he could see that – and the farmer carefully picked her up and put her on the passenger seat and turned for home.

"I reckon this bird's been shot, Emma," he said to his wife as he brought the duck into the kitchen. "It's a funny thing, but about an hour ago Rory here came into the milking-parlour whining and whimpering as though he was worried stiff about something."

"He knew his friend was in trouble, you mean, Jim?"

"Could be. Animals know things we couldn't know. Hold her a minute while I have a look at this wing."

Gently he stretched it.

"Don't think anything's broken," he said. "Ah, look, I see. I was right, someone's had a bang at her. There's a little cluster of shot right in the angle of the wing joint, can you see, little black things—just under the skin."

154

He looked at his watch.

"The vet won't have finished his evening surgery yet," he said. "Come on, duck, off we go again."

The vet had extracted all the pellets, and then bandaged Damaris right round the middle, pinning both wings to her sides. Still woozy from the anaesthetic, she spent that night in a large cardboard box beside the Aga.

"We don't want her flapping about, not for a day or two," the vet had said. "Give things time to heal. She's been lucky."

By morning Damaris felt a different duck. Her injured wing was stiff and sore certainly, but she was safe and at home and well looked after. The farmer and his wife fed her and fussed over her, and even Tess bothered to look into the box and say "Better?"

As for Rory, his concern for his friend was so obvious that the farmer decided to excuse him from duty.

The farmer's wife came and lifted Damaris out of the cardboard box: she had lined it with newspapers that were by now extremely messy, and she replaced them with a fresh layer.

It so happened that one of these was a

Large White boar Championship at th

magazine, an old copy of the *Pig Breeders'
Gazette*, and when Damaris was replaced
in the box, she noticed what she was
about to sit on.

The print, of course, meant nothing to
her – "Large White boar wins Supreme
Championship at the Royal Show" was
to her a lot of little black squiggles – but
the picture below immediately caught
her eye.

It was the spitting image of the
General.

Something clicked in Damaris's
unusually large brain.

Here was a way to communicate with
the farmer!

Not by word of mouth – she couldn't
speak to him.

Not by her actions – she had tried
flying away and calling to him to follow,
but in vain.

157

But how about a pictorial message?
Show him the picture!

"Rory," she said, "look in here."

Rory peered into the box.

"It's a picture of a pig," he said.

"Yes. Can you get it out?"

Damaris stood to one side as the
sheepdog put his head into the box and
carefully picked up the magazine in his
mouth.

"Put it on the floor, pig upwards," she
said.

He did.

"Now, do you see what I'm getting
at?"

"No."

"Listen then."

Rory listened as Damaris explained her
idea.

Then he said, "Brilliant! But are they
clever enough to get the message?"

158

"You've got it," said Damaris, "and
they're meant to be more intelligent than
any dog."

"Or even any pig."

"And certainly any duck."

"Except one," said Rory proudly.

The farmer's wife came into the
kitchen.

"Go on, Rory," quacked Damaris
softly.

Rory began to bark excitedly. He bounced about beside the *Pig Breeders' Gazette*, putting a paw on the picture, scratching at it, pointing his muzzle at it, doing everything in his power to get the woman to look at it.

She did.

"Whatever's the matter, Rory?" she said.

The farmer came in.

"Whatever's the matter with Rory?" he said.

"He's trying to tell us something."

At that moment Damaris joined in. She could not flap her wings because of the bandaging, but she quacked as loudly as she could. The farmer's wife lifted her out of the cardboard box and put her down on the floor beside the magazine, and Damaris began to tap with her bill upon the picture of the Supreme

160

Champion Large White.

"She's trying to tell us something, too," she said. "About our pigs, it must be."

"There you go again, Emma," the farmer said. "Trying to tell me that these two know where the pigs are."

"Remember what you said, Jim. 'Animals know things we couldn't know.' Those were your very words."

"Yes, but I was talking about a dog like Rory. There's no such thing as a clever duck, not outside of a children's story book."

7. Market Day

"Anyway," said the farmer, "I'd best be off on my usual search. I must have looked in almost every field in this valley. Someone must have them shut up somewhere."

"You're just taking Tess?" his wife said.

"Yes."

But as he went out of the kitchen, Rory followed and at his heels Damaris came waddling as fast as she could.

The farmer's wife went to the front door to see them off. The dogs had as usual jumped up into the bed of the truck. Damaris was standing waiting by the passenger door.

"You'll have to take her, Jim," the farmer's wife said.

"She won't be able to see anything, she's too short."

"You'll just have to stop every so often and lift her out and let her have a look round. If she quacks and Rory barks, like they've just been doing, I reckon you're getting warm. Try all the villages in turn."

Some time after the pick-up truck had gone off down the farm road, a cattle lorry drove into Mr Crook's yard. It was market day in a distant town, and the dealer reckoned he had waited long enough. Whoever owns these pigs, he said to himself, must have given up hope by now.

Meanwhile the farmer had driven in turn to the villages of Muddlebury, Muddlechester, Upper Muddle and Lower Muddle. Near each he had stopped and, feeling a fool, had lifted Damaris out. But she had made no sound. Each time, Rory had barked, but Damaris remained silent.

The dog barks at the smell of pigs, any pigs, the farmer thought, but will the duck only quack at the right pigs? What am I saying? The duck knows more than the dog? I'm beginning to believe it.

In a lane outside Muddlehampton, not far from the River Muddle, he stopped and lifted Damaris out once more.

Immediately she began to quack loudly and to struggle wildly in his arms. Hearing her, Rory let out a volley of

164

barks and Tess, of course, joined in.

"What's all that racket, boss?" said the haulier to Mr Crook as they raised the tail-board behind the pigs and clamped it shut, and at that moment they saw a pick-up truck come to a stop in the yard gateway, blocking it.

From it jumped a man holding in his arms a bandaged duck and followed by two sheepdogs. The dogs were barking and growling, the duck was quacking madly, and the man, who looked angry, walked up to Mr Crook and said, "What have you got in that lorry?"

"Mind your own business," said the dealer.

"It *is* my business," said the farmer.

"You've got a pedigree Large White boar and seven sows in there, haven't you?"

The haulier's jaw dropped.

"Here," he said, "how did you know that?"

"There's something else I know too," said the farmer.

He took a notebook out of his pocket.

"Now then," he said to the dealer, "here are all the numbers on the ear-tags

of these pigs. Let's have a look and see if they match, shall we?"

Mr Crook knew when he was beaten.

"Hang on a bit," he said to his haulier, and he took the farmer across the yard to his office.

"Am I pleased to see you, sir!" he said. "I've been keeping those pigs safe, hoping someone would claim them. Couldn't afford to keep them any longer, you know – eating me out of house and home. Just loading them up to send to a friend of mine that's got a bit of rough ground . . ."

"Don't bother spinning me a cock-and-bull story about it," said the farmer. "I know the dates of the markets. I'll tell you where you're sending them and that's straight to my farm. You'll pay the haulage of course."

"They've cost me a lot already," said Mr Crook sullenly.

"And they'd have earned you a nice lot too if I hadn't turned up," said the farmer.

"How did you know where to come?"

The farmer looked at the dealer.

Then he looked at Damaris.

Then he looked at a shotgun, propped in the corner of the office.

Then he suddenly knew, beyond a shadow of a doubt, what had happened.

"The duck told me," he said. "I'll send you the vet's bill."

Mr Crook mopped his face with a large spotted handkerchief. "No need for us to say anything to anybody else about all this business, is there, sir?" he said.

"No need at all," said the farmer. "And I'll tell the duck to keep quiet about it too."

8.   Clever Duck!

"There's no place like home," grunted
Mrs Stout to Mrs Portly as the pigs made
their way down the tail-board of the
cattle lorry and through the freshly
mended gate into their old paddock.

"Quite right, dear," said Mrs Portly.

"Journey's end," said Mrs O'Bese,
"and it was a miserable old journey, so it
was."

"Hear, hear!" said Mrs Chubby, Mrs
Tubby, Mrs Swagbelly and Mrs Roly-Poly.

Only Firingclose General Lord Nicholas of Winningshot said nothing. The promised land had not lived up to its promise, and for once he thought it wise to keep his mouth shut. What's more, he soon found that he no longer had one of the two pig huts to himself, for the sows took over both of them, and grumbled loudly when he meekly tried to push in, so that he often found himself sleeping outside. A male chauvinist pig he may once have been, but now he was to his wives just a boring old boar and they did not hesitate to tell him so.

Two months later, however, the General had the paddock to himself. His wives had all been moved to a range of farrowing houses to await the birth of their children.

Damaris felt sorry for the boar. Once her wing was fully healed, she flew over now and again for a chat. Not that she got a word in edgewise. The General had lost much of his authority, but none of his gift of the gab. He appeared quite unaware of the duck's part in the rescue, as indeed were all the sows except one.

Maybe it had something to do with Mrs O'Bese's Celtic blood, but she alone mentioned it when Damaris went visiting the expectant mothers.

"Sure and it was you that found us, wasn't it, duck?" she said. "I knew you were the clever one, right from the start. 'If you don't know what an ignoramus is,' you said, 'then you must be one.' Begorrah, you could have knocked me down with a duck's feather. And I never thought much of ducks before."

"Why not?" said Damaris.

"Too stupid, I thought. Don't know anything."

"Actually," said Damaris, "I never thought much of pigs before."

"Why not?" said Mrs O'Bese.

"Too clever by half. Think they know everything."

Mrs O'Bese gave a fusillade of little grunts that sounded like "Ha! Ha! Ha! Ha!"

"I know one thing, duck," she said. "I like you, so I do. Good luck to you."

"Thanks," said Damaris, "and I hope all your troubles will be little ones."

Which they were, because before long all the sows farrowed.

Most had eight, nine or ten piglets, but Mrs O'Bese, just to be different, gave birth to no less than thirteen little half-Irish babies.

"Let us only hope," she said, "that they don't grow up to be as long-winded as their dada, or it will be an unlucky number."

"I like that Irish sow," said Damaris to Rory. They were having one of their evening conversations out in the orchard, Rory lying in the grass, Damaris squatting beside him.

"She's the best of a bad lot," said Rory, "but none of them has changed really. They still patronize all the other animals on the farm. They still think they're the greatest and they don't hide the fact."

"Look at those two, Emma," said the farmer to his wife, as side by side they leaned against the orchard gate, enjoying the end of the day.

"It's the strangest friendship, Jim," she said.

"That's the strangest duck," he said. "I've said it many times before, I know, but she saved us a packet of money. We'd never have seen our pigs again, and that dealer would have been laughing. She found them, all by herself."

"And could have lost her life."

"Yes. Why should a duck worry about pigs? She goes visiting them, you know. I saw her today, quacking away to that

old Irish sow and the sow grunting back at her. Look at her now, bending Rory's ear about something or other. I'd dearly love to understand what animals say to one another."

"Look at the farmer and his wife chatting away, Rory," Damaris said. "I'd dearly love to understand what humans say to one another."

176

"That," said Rory, "is one thing you're
never going to be able to do. I can
understand the odd word – 'Come by!',
'Away to me!', 'Down', 'Stay' – that sort
of thing. But most of what they say is
gibberish."

He got up and moved towards the two
people, Damaris waddling behind.

"Listen," he said. "They'll say

something when we reach them," and when they did, the man patted him and said a couple of words.

"I got that," Rory said. "He's telling me I'm a good dog."

The woman bent down and stroked Damaris's brown-and-white plumage, and she too spoke two words.

"What did she say to me?" asked Damaris.

"Haven't a clue," replied Rory, as the farmer's wife said once more "Clever duck!"

The
Swoose

DICK KING-SMITH

The Swoose

Illustrated by Judy Brown

1.

"Mum," said Fitzherbert. "Why do I look
different from all the other goslings on
the farm?"

He did, there was no denying it. He
was larger than the rest, his feet were
bigger, and his neck was longer.

"You *are* different," said his mother.

"Because I'm an only child, d'you
mean?"

The other geese all had five or six goslings apiece, but Fitzherbert alone had hatched from his mother's clutch of eggs.

"An only child in more ways than one," she said. "I doubt if there's another bird like you in the whole wide world. All these other youngsters will grow up to be ordinary common or garden geese, but not you, Fitzherbert my boy."

"But I'm a goose like you, Mum, aren't I?" said Fitzherbert.

"No," said his mother, "you are not." She lowered her voice.

"You," she said softly, "are a swoose."

Fitzherbert coiled his long neck backwards into the shape of an S.

"A what?" he cried.

"Sssssssh!" hissed his mother, and she waddled off to a distant corner of the

186

farmyard, away from all the other geese.

Fitzherbert hurried after her.

"What did you say I was?" he asked.

His mother looked around to make
sure they were out of earshot of the rest
of the flock, and then she said, "Now
listen carefully. What I am about to tell
you must be a secret between you and
me, always. D'you understand?"

"Yes, Mum," said Fitzherbert.

"You are old enough now to be told," said his mother, "why you are unlike all the other goslings on the farm. They are the children of a number of geese, but all of them have the same father."

"The old grey gander, you mean?"

"Yes."

"But isn't he my father too?"

"No."

"Then who is?"

"Your father," said Fitzherbert's mum, and a dreamy look came over her face as she spoke, "is neither old nor grey. Your father is young and strong and as white as the driven snow. Never shall I forget the day we met!"

"Where was that, Mum?"

"It was by the river. I had gone down by myself for a swim, when suddenly he appeared, high in the sky above. Oh, the music of his great wings! It was love at first flight! Then he landed on the surface in a shower of spray and swam towards me."

"But I don't get it, Mum," said Fitzherbert. "What was he? Another sort of goose?"

"No," said his mother. "He was a swan."

"What's that?"

"A swan is the most beautiful of all

birds, and your father was the most
beautiful of all swans."

"What was his name?"

"He didn't say. He was a mute swan."

Fitzherbert thought about all this for a
while.

Then he said, "So I might be the only
swoose in the world?"

"Yes."

"There aren't any other swooses?"

"Sweese."

"Eh?"

"When there's more than one goose, you say geese. So more than one swoose would be sweese."

"But there isn't more than one. Just me. You just said so, didn't you?"

As mothers do, Fitzherbert's mum

became fed up with his constant questions.

"Oh, run away and play," she said.

But playing with the other goslings wasn't a lot of fun for Fitzherbert. Already they had noticed that he was different. They poked fun at him, calling him Bigfeet or Snakyneck, and they wouldn't let him join in their games.

Time passed, and Fitzherbert began to grow his adult feathers. Often, as he thought of his father swooping down from the sky on whistling wings, he flapped his own and wished that he too could fly. Farmyard geese like his mother and the rest couldn't, he knew – they were too heavy-bodied to get off the ground. But swans could. How about a swoose? And the more he thought about his father, the more he wanted to meet

him. So one day he decided to go down to the river by himself. He would say nothing to his mother about it, but just set off when she wasn't looking.

He had never before been out of the farmyard, and he was not at all sure what the river looked like, let alone where it was, but luck was on his side. He walked across a couple of fields and there it was, in front of him!

Fitzherbert looked at the wide stretch of water, winking and gleaming in the sunlight and chuckling to itself as it flowed along. Never in his life had he swum upon anything but the duckpond at the farm, but this – this is the place for swimming, he thought, and he waddled down the bank and pushed off.

He paddled about in midstream, looking up at the sky, hoping that a

snow-white shape would come gliding down to greet him.

Instead he suddenly turned to see a whole armada of snow-white shapes sailing silently downstream towards him. There must have been at least twenty swans, all making for this stranger who dared to swim upon their river. Their wings were curved in excitement, and the look in their black eyes was far from friendly.

Oh, thought Fitzherbert, as the fleet of swans approached, all now grunting and hissing angrily, oh dear, I really must fly!

2.

As Fitzherbert swam hastily away from his pursuers, he spread his wings and beat them madly on the water in an effort to increase his speed. Harder and harder he flapped, and then he felt his body lift a little so that now, instead of swimming, he was slapping his broad webs on the surface in a kind of clumsy run.

Suddenly he was airborne, and the swans, satisfied that they had seen off the stranger, did not trouble to follow.

It wasn't much of a flight, that first effort. For perhaps a quarter of a mile, Fitzherbert laboured along only a few yards above the water, and then, tired out by his efforts, flopped back down into the river. He looked anxiously around, but to his great relief, there was no sign of the swans. Nasty, bad-tempered creatures, he said to himself. I wasn't doing them any harm. Why, my dad might have been one of that lot. I don't know that I want to meet him after all.

He swam on, looking about him with interest. He could see other birds on the water – different sorts of duck, and moorhen, and coot – and there was a sudden brilliant flash of colour as a

kingfisher darted across. There were
people on the river too, in rowing-boats
and punts, and one very long thin craft
shot by with eight large young men
pulling at their oars, while a ninth much
smaller man steered and shouted at them
through a kind of tube held to his
mouth.

"In! Out! In! Out!" he called, and the blades dipped and rose as one.

Fitzherbert drifted dreamily with the current, enjoying the sunlit scene, when suddenly a sharp voice cried, "Avast there, you landlubber, or you'll run us down!"

Startled, the swoose looked down to meet the angry gaze of a small water-vole.

"Oh sorry!" said Fitzherbert. "I'm afraid I wasn't looking where I was going."

The vole did not answer, but swam to the bank. Fitzherbert followed.

"I suppose you couldn't tell me?" he said.

The vole turned at the mouth of his burrow.

"Tell you what?" he said.

"Where I'm going?"

The vole stared beadily at the swoose.

"Are you feather-brained?" he said.

"No, I'm Fitzherbert."

The water-vole shook his blunt head as though to clear it.

"Tell us something," he said. "You come sailing along without any regard

for the rule of the river, and then you go
and talk a load of rubbish. Anyways, I
never in my life set eyes on a bird like
you before. What are you?"

"I'm a . . ." began Fitzherbert, and
then he thought, oh no, I promised Mum
I wouldn't tell.

"I can't really say," he replied.

"You don't know what you are," said
the vole. "You don't know where you're
going. Next thing, you'll be telling me
you don't know what river this is."

"No. I don't."

"Then you don't know the name of
that town you can see, down at the end
of the reach?"

"No."

"Nor the castle on the hill above it?"

"No."

"Nor who lives in that castle?"

"No," said Fitzherbert. "I've never

been outside our farmyard before. But I'd be very grateful if you'd tell me."

"You're lucky, young fellow," said the vole. "You've come to the right chap. Now, if you'd asked a moorhen, or worse, a duck, you'd have been wasting your breath. But there isn't much that I don't know about this here stretch of the Thames."

"The what?"

"The Thames. That's the name of this river. Most famous river in all England, I'd say. And that town yonder is Windsor, and that's Windsor Castle above it. Now then, surely you know who lives there?"

"No."

"Why, the Queen, of course."

"Oh," said Fitzherbert. "What's a queen?" he said.

The water-vole sighed deeply.

"You're a bright one," he said. "She's only the most important person in the land, that's all."

At this point a pair of swans appeared in midstream.

Fitzherbert backed into a clump of reeds and kept his head down.

"Now d'you see those swans?" said the vole. "They belong to the Queen, they do, like every other swan in the country. Royal birds, swans are."

Oh, thought Fitzherbert, I wonder if sweese are? I bet she's never seen one.

"This queen," he said. "What's she called?"

"Victoria. She's been Queen for donkey's years, she has."

"Donkey's ears?" said Fitzherbert.

"Why, 'tis ages ago she lost her husband."

"Couldn't she find him again?"

The water-vole sighed and continued.

"And ever since she's shut herself up in that castle. Always dressed in black, she is. The Widow of Windsor, they call her."

"How do you know all these things?" asked Fitzherbert.

"I keep my ears open," said the water-vole. "Windsor folk come out boating on the river and I listen to all the latest gossip."

"She doesn't sound very happy, this queen," said Fitzherbert.

"She isn't. Grumpy old thing, from all accounts."

"Perhaps she needs cheering up."

"Easier said than done. Anybody tries making a joke, she says, 'We are not amused'," said the vole, and with that he vanished into his burrow.

A moment later he stuck his head out again.

"She might be amused at you," he said. "Why don't you pay her a visit?"

Why don't I? thought the swoose.

"I will," he said, "and I'll come back and tell you all about it."

Then it occurred to him that there were probably a great many water-voles living beside the Thames.

"So can you tell me your name, please?" he said.

"Alph," said the vole, and he disappeared once more.

3.

Dressed all in black, Queen Victoria
stood at an upper window in Windsor
Castle and looked down at the courtyard
below. In the centre of this courtyard
was a perfect square of brilliantly green
grass, a lawn that was not only
personally mown by the Royal Head
Gardener, but afterwards finely

manicured by a number of under-gardeners. No other feet were allowed upon this lawn, save those of the Queen's pet dogs and of the footman who tidied up after them with an elegant brass shovel.

But now it seemed there was a large shape, right in the centre of the square of green.

The Queen held out a hand.

"Our pince-nez," she said to her Lady of the Bedchamber, and when these were brought, she fitted them upon the bridge of the Royal nose.

For some moments she stared down, and then she said, "And what, pray, is that?"

"It is a bird, ma'am," said the Lady of the Bedchamber.

"We can see that," said Queen Victoria. "We are not blind. See that it is

215

removed immediately. Whatever is it doing on our grass?" and she turned away from the window.

The Lady of the Bedchamber heaved a sigh of relief that she'd avoided having to answer the Queen's last question. She could see plainly what the bird had that moment done on the grass.

"That's better!" said Fitzherbert as he waddled away from the large squelchy mess he had just made.

He was feeling pretty pleased with himself. Everything had gone swimmingly. He had swum on down the Thames, keeping well away from swans, and stopping every now and then to feed on juicy water-plants. It was late in the day before he came to the town, so he decided to wait till next morning before visiting the castle.

At dawn Fitzherbert looked up to see
its looming walls and towers. Good job
sweese can fly, he thought, and he took
off and flew up the hill.

The town of Windsor was still asleep
and its streets were as yet empty of the
busy horse-drawn traffic. Only a

milkman driving his cart with its load of
brass-bound wooden churns noticed a
large bird fly up Castle Hill and over the
turrets of the Henry VIII Gate.

This, Fitzherbert's second flight, was
altogether a much more successful effort.
Even so, he tired rapidly, and, seeing a

square of grass in an inner courtyard, he
landed thankfully upon it. It was a crash-
landing that knocked the wind out of
him, and for some time he lay and
gasped for breath.

Finally recovered, he looked about
him. Then he saw a movement at an
upper window. Someone was looking
down at him. He could not see the figure
clearly, but it appeared to be dressed in
black!

220

If that's the Queen, thought Fitzherbert, I'd better make myself comfortable before I meet her. He stood up and suited his actions to his words.

"That's better!" he said, and he waddled off slowly towards the nearest door.

The Lady of the Bedchamber lost no time in contacting the Lord Steward of Her Majesty's Household.

"There's a large bird," she said to him, "in the Queen's private courtyard, and she wants it removed immediately."

"What sort of a bird?" asked the Lord Steward.

"I don't know," said the Lady of the Bedchamber. "It was something like a swan. But, then again, it was something like a goose."

The Lord Steward of Her Majesty's

Household sent for the Ornithologist Royal, the man who looked after the Queen's birds.

"There's a large bird," he said, "in Her Majesty's private courtyard. Get rid of it, will you?"

"What sort of a bird?" asked the Ornithologist Royal.

"Part swan, part goose, apparently."

"Part swan, part goose!" murmured the Ornithologist Royal excitedly to himself as he hurried to do the Lord Steward's bidding. "Could it be . . . ? Could it be?"

When the door into the courtyard opened, Fitzherbert was disappointed to see a man emerge. He seemed a nice man, however, for he produced some pieces of bread which he offered to the swoose. But no sooner had Fitzherbert begun to eat them than he was grabbed,

his wings pinioned to his sides, and he
was carried, kicking and struggling,
away.

"It is! It is!" said the Ornithologist
Royal as he listened to his captive's cries
of protest, a blend of the grunting bark of
an angry swan and the cackling of an
outraged goose. He carried Fitzherbert to
the Royal Menagerie, where all manner

of creatures were housed, presented as gifts to the Queen by visiting foreign rulers.

"It is!" said the Ornithologist Royal again as he feasted his eyes upon Fitzherbert, now shut in a large cage. "I had heard tales of such a bird, but never thought to see one! It is a swoose!"

"That bird," said the Lord Steward of Her Majesty's Household later. "Have you dealt with it?"

"Yes," said the Ornithologist Royal.

"What was it?"

"It is a swoose!" said the Ornithologist Royal. "A cross between a swan and a goose! A *rara avis* indeed! Her Majesty should be told."

The Lord Steward of Her Majesty's Household remembered enough of his Latin to say to the Lady of the

225

Bedchamber, "It's a rare bird, the one that was in the Queen's courtyard. Called a swoose apparently. Her Majesty should be told."

Nervously, for the Queen did not like to be told things, preferring that people should not speak until they were spoken to, the Lady of the Bedchamber approached her sovereign.

"Forgive me, Your Majesty," she said, "but that bird, that you saw earlier this morning . . ."

"Well?" said the Queen, her face set in its usual grim mode.

"I am given to understand, ma'am, that it is a swoose."

"A what?"

"A swoose, ma'am."

To the great astonishment of the Lady of the Bedchamber, something that might almost have been called a small

226

smile appeared on the Royal face. Never
in all the many years she had served at
court had the Lady of the Bedchamber
seen such a thing.

"A swoose," said Queen Victoria.
"Why, surely that must be part swan,
part goose!"

"Perhaps Your Majesty might care to

see the creature?" said the Lady of the Bedchamber.

"We would," said the Queen.

So it was that Fitzherbert, puzzled and angry at being shut in, saw the doors of the Royal Menagerie opened by a pair of bewigged footmen and a procession enter.

Followed by the Lord Steward, the Ornithologist Royal and the Lady of the

Bedchamber, and attended by the Lord Chamberlain, the Comptroller of Her Majesty's Household, the Master of the Horse and several Ladies-in-Waiting, came a short dumpy figure, dressed all in black.

For some time Queen Victoria stared at Fitzherbert without speaking. Naturally no one else spoke.

Then the Queen said, "Are we right?

Is this bird indeed half-swan and half-goose?"

"Your Majesty is perfectly correct," said the Ornithologist Royal.

"And it is a rarity?"

"Indeed, ma'am."

"We do not like to see it so imprisoned. Open the door of its cage."

"But, ma'am . . ." began the
Ornithologist Royal, fearing that the bird
might misbehave itself in some way,
might even (dreadful thought) peck the
Royal ankles.

"Do as we say," snapped the Queen,
"and look sharp about it," and the
Ornithologist Royal looked very sharp
indeed.

Fitzherbert could, of course,
understand nothing of the medley of
sounds that the humans made.
However, it was clear to him that, thanks
to the Queen, he was to be a prisoner no
longer, and he thought that he should
show his gratitude.

With measured tread he walked out of
the cage and stood at attention before the

Queen. Then he slowly uncurled his long
neck and laid his head upon the ground
at the very feet of the monarch in a
gesture that was the nearest he could
come to a courtly bow.

To the amazement of the Lord Steward
of Her Majesty's Household and the
Ornithologist Royal and the Lady of the
Bedchamber and the Lord Chamberlain
and the Comptroller of Her Majesty's
Household and the Master of the Horse
and the Ladies-in-Waiting and the two

bewigged footmen, none of whom
recalled ever seeing such a sight before,
Queen Victoria looked down at the
swoose and smiled broadly.

"We are amused," said the Widow of
Windsor.

4.

The news that something had made the
Queen smile for the first time in a quarter
of a century, or, in other words, since the
death of her husband Prince Albert,
spread like wildfire among the courtiers
at Windsor Castle. Not only had she
smiled once, but had continued to do so,
and had even spoken quite pleasantly to
a number of people. More, she had
exchanged her widow's cap of black for
one of white lace, and all because of that
swoose!

"It's all so beautifully timed," the Lord
Steward of Her Majesty's Household said
to the Lady of the Bedchamber. "Next
year it's the Queen's Golden Jubilee as
you know, when the whole kingdom will
be celebrating her fifty years on the

236

throne, and she will have to go about and show herself to the people. How pleased they will be to see her wearing a happy face again after all those years of gloom. The greatest care must be taken of that bird."

Unfortunately, it wasn't.

The very next morning, the Ornithologist Royal came in armed with a large pair of scissors. He intended to clip the flight feathers of one of the swoose's wings, a painless operation which would render the bird incapable of flight. Little did he guess that Fitzherbert had plans of his own.

First, despite having been released from his cage the previous evening on the Queen's orders, he had been shut up again as soon as she had gone, and this he did not like.

Second, he was longing to tell the

238

water-vole all about his audience with
Queen Victoria.

So the moment the Ornithologist Royal
opened the cage, Fitzherbert pushed past
him and made his way as fast as he could
along a corridor and out through a door.

"Stop! Stop!" cried the Ornithologist Royal, hurrying after him, scissors in hand, and then could only stand and watch in horror as the swoose took wing and flew away towards the Thames.

Fitzherbert flew upriver, trying to remember whereabouts it was that he had met the vole, when suddenly he saw him swimming across a little backwater.

"Alph!" he cried, and swooping down, landed with a great splash. He looked around, but could only see a couple of moorhens that squawked angrily at him from the rushes.

Then he saw a blunt brown head break surface.

"Alph!" he cried again. "Remember me?"

"How could I forget you?" said the vole sharply. "First time we met, you nearly ran me down, and now you drop

out of the sky almost on top of me.
You're a clumsy great hummock and no
mistake."

"Sorry, Alph," said Fitzherbert. "I was
in a hurry to tell you. I've seen the
Queen! And what d'you think – she
smiled at me!"

"Fancy!" said Alph.

He swam to the bank, and climbed out
and shook himself.

"Wonder why?" he said.

"I don't really know," said Fitzherbert. "She seemed to like me. And they were all very pleased. Everyone was ever so nice to me."

"They didn't shut you up then?" said Alph.

"Well, yes, they did, but I escaped."

"What for?"

"Why, to come and find you and thank you."

"What for?"

"For suggesting I should visit the Queen. It was a great idea. I must be getting back now, I dare say Her Majesty's missing me, wouldn't you think?"

For a moment the water-vole did not answer. He sat on his haunches, combing his very small round ears with his forepaws. Then he fixed his very small beady eyes on the swoose.

"I hope you know what you're doing, young fellow," he said. "It's all very well being the Queen's pet, but what if she gets fed up with you, eh?"

'Well, then I suppose she'd just let me go."

"She might," said Alph. "Or she might not. There's plenty of meat on you from what I can see. You don't want to end up like that, do you?"

"End up like what?" asked Fitzherbert.

"Eaten," said Alph. "At Windsor," and down his burrow he went.

5.

Meanwhile, back at the castle, panic reigned.

Everyone now knew that the swoose had flown away. Everyone, that is, except the Queen, and all were waiting, horrified, for the moment when she would find out.

The Ornithologist Royal in particular was in a cold sweat. He had let the bird escape. He, everyone agreed, would lose his job.

So it was with a great sigh of relief that the worried man saw Fitzherbert come winging back over the battlements to land once more in the inner courtyard. Armed with his scissors, he hurried out.

As he did so, an upper window was flung open and a commanding voice

called out, "Stop! And wait for us!"

The Ornithologist Royal stopped and
waited, his heart in his mouth. What if
the bird should take off again?

But Fitzherbert had no intention of
doing so. To begin with, the flight to
Alph and back had been quite tiring, and
secondly, though he did not understand

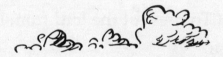

the words, he recognized the note of
command in the Royal tones.

In a little while Queen Victoria
emerged from a side door into the
courtyard, leaning upon the arm of the
Lady of the Bedchamber.

The Ornithologist Royal was a tall
man, but he felt very small at sight of the

dumpy little Queen's frowning face.

"What," she said, "are you doing with those scissors?"

"If you please, Your Majesty," said the Ornithologist Royal, "I was intending to pinion the bird."

"To pinion it?"

"To cut the flight feathers of one wing, ma'am."

"With what object?"

"To prevent the bird from leaving you."

"Leaving *us*?" said the Queen. "Flying away, from *our* presence, do you mean? What an absurd idea! You will put those scissors away, sir, or it will be you who is leaving."

Soon the whole court knew that, far from being chopped off, the feathers of the Queen's pet swoose must on no account

252

be so much as ruffled. He was to have the choicest food, such as fresh young vegetables from the kitchen gardens, brought to him by the Royal Head Gardener in person, and Scotch oatmeal porridge served by the Queen's manservant, John Brown.

In addition, the Royal Head Gardener's little daughter was appointed Swoosegirl-in-Waiting, to take Fitzherbert for daily walks in Windsor Great Park. By night, however, he was still shut in the Royal Menagerie for his own safety (for foxes, the Ornithologist Royal was sure, would be no respecters of sweese), but the Queen came in each evening to see her pet. Fitzherbert would make his bow, the Queen would smile, and everyone would heave a sigh of relief at the welcome change that had come over the crusty old lady.

At first Fitzherbert found the nights
trying. By day there were so many
people making a fuss of him, but at night
he was lonely. None of the other inmates
of the menagerie such as parrots or
monkeys bothered to talk to him, and he

thought how nice it would be to have a chat with someone like Alph.

How pleasant it was then to hear a friendly voice one evening, just after the Queen and her company had left.

A cultured voice it was, a little singsong in tone, and altogether quite unlike the country voice of the water-vole, though in fact it belonged to another rodent.

"How are you settling in, may one ask?" said the voice, and Fitzherbert looked up to see that the speaker was a rat.

He had come across rats before, in the farmyard, ugly-looking creatures with rough brown coats, but this one was quite different.

To begin with, it was smaller and slenderer than a farm rat, with large thin ears and the longest of tails, longer even than its whole body. And second, that body was clothed in the glossiest of blue-black fur.

Altogether it was the most elegant animal, Fitzherbert thought, and he answered politely, "Quite well, thank you."

"Allow me to introduce myself," said the black rat. "My name is Maharanee."

"Fitzherbert," said the swoose.

"A noble-sounding name," said Maharanee.

"So's yours," said Fitzherbert. "It sounds foreign."

"So it is," said the black rat. "Her Majesty, as you may know, is also Empress of India, and her loyal subjects within the raj often send her gifts of animals. I stowed away with such a shipload, believing my proper place to be at court."

"I don't quite understand," said Fitzherbert.

"I myself am of Royal blood. I was born in a palace, so it is fitting that I should associate myself with Her Majesty. Maharanee, you see, means 'Great Queen'."

"Oh," said Fitzherbert. "So you're a favourite of hers too, are you?"

"I wouldn't exactly say that," replied Maharanee. "The English, you know, are less than friendly towards our brown cousins and are apt to tar black rats with the same brush. I tend therefore to keep a low profile. But you certainly seem to have taken Her Majesty's fancy. You're quite the Royal pet."

Until she gets fed up with me, thought Fitzherbert, and then suddenly remembered that that was what Alph had said.

"Look here, Maharanee," he said. "You don't suppose she'd ever . . . eat me, do you?"

The black rat looked at the swoose consideringly, and strangely, she too echoed Alph's words.

"She might," she said. "Or she might not. But if you are ever to be on the menu, I shall hear about it. I spend a good deal of time in the castle kitchens. Rely upon me to give you warning, Fitzherbert my friend."

So the time passed pleasantly for the swoose. Not only did he enjoy the favour of the Queen, with all the benefits that came with it; but now he had two friends.

At night he had long and interesting conversations with the much-travelled Maharanee, and as often as he liked, he

flew upriver for a chat with the
homespun Alph. To see the swoose go
gave the Ornithologist Royal fifty fits at
first, but gradually he became confident
that the bird would always return.

All went well until the Head Cook and Bottlewasher at Windsor Castle reached retirement age and was replaced.

The black rat arrived in Fitzherbert's cage one evening in high excitement.

"What do you think!" she said. "There is a French chef in the kitchen! No more stodgy, unimaginative English cooking. Now we shall see food fit for a Queen and leftovers fit for a Maharanee! There is nothing that a good chef cannot cook."

Except sweese, I hope, thought Fitzherbert.

6.

Soon after this, some foreign cousins of the Queen were due to stay at the castle, and the new chef was instructed to plan a modest ten-course dinner for the visitors.

"And make sure that the main course is something really spectacular, said the Lord Steward.

The French chef sought the advice of the Queen's Butler.

"Is there something," he asked, "that only Royalty may eat, *monsieur*?"

The Queen's Butler thought for a moment.

"Why yes," he said. "There is. Swan. Royal birds, swans are. No one else is allowed to eat them. There are plenty down there on the Thames."

Roast swan and all the trimmings, thought the chef. That will indeed be *spectaculaire*!

All might yet have been well had not the chef lost his way in the many halls and corridors of the castle. One morning he took from his knife-rack the largest of his carving knives, closely watched, though he did not know this, by an elegant blue-black creature crouching beneath a dresser.

He fingered the knife's edge, and then, shaking his head at its bluntness, set off to have it sharpened at the Armoury. However, he failed to understand the directions given him, and became confused in the maze of passages.

Opening a door, he found himself in
an enclosed courtyard, in the centre of
which was a perfect square of brilliantly
green grass.

Right in the centre of it was a large
shape.

The chef's hand tightened on his carving knife.

"*Voilà!*" he said softly. "No need to go to the river. The bird has come to me!"

Fitzherbert was dozing, a little tired after his daily walk. The Swoosegirl-in-Waiting had gone home to tea, and the Ornithologist Royal had not yet arrived to take the Queen's pet to the menagerie for the night.

Suddenly the swoose was woken by the voice of Maharanee.

"Fly, Fitzherbert, fly!" squealed the black rat.

Opening his eyes, the swoose saw a man approaching, a man dressed all in white and wearing a tall white hat, a man brandishing a huge knife!

At that very moment, a door opposite opened, and out of it, supported by her

270

Lady of the Bedchamber, came Queen Victoria.

In his terror, Fitzherbert totally disregarded Maharanee's instructions. Indeed, he completely forgot that he possessed his wild father's powers of flight and reverted to his mother's farmyard waddle.

Grunting, barking, cackling at the top of his voice, he hastened towards the Queen and turned and stood in front of her, his eyes fixed in horror on that dreadful knife that was destined, he was sure, for his throat.

Then, drawn by the terrible noise that the swoose was making, a host of people appeared and fell upon the wretched chef and dragged him away.

Later that evening, when all had been explained (and the luckless chef sent

hurriedly back to France), the Queen
came with her company into the
menagerie. They brought a gilded chair
for her, and she sat and looked at her
swoose.

"What courage!" she said quietly.
"Not only did he sound the alarm, but
he stood before us, thinking that we
were to be murdered. He believed that
he was saving us!"

Everyone looked at everyone else, but
nobody said anything.

"We shall reward him for his bravery,"
said the Queen, and those nearest could
see that her old eyes were twinkling.

"Open the door of the cage," she
commanded, and they opened it.

Fitzherbert stepped forward and stood
at attention before the monarch's chair,
and then, as always, lowered his head to
the floor.

The Queen looked round at her courtiers and she positively grinned.

Then she raised her silver-headed, ebony walking-stick and with it she lightly touched Fitzherbert upon one shoulder.

"I dub thee Knight!" said Queen Victoria in a loud voice. "Arise, Sir Swoose!"

And slowly, proudly, to a burst of clapping from the smiling company of watchers, Fitzherbert arose.